Read-Along
STORYBOOK AND CD

Wreck-It Ralph is a video-game Bad Guy who wants to prove he can be a hero. To find out what happens, read along with me in your book. You will know it's time to turn the page when you hear this sound. . . .

Let's begin now.

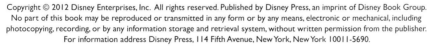

Printed in the United States of America

First Edition 10 9 8 7 6 5 4 3 2

V381-8386-5-12292

Library of Congress Control Number: 2012933315

ISBN: 978-1-4231-6061-8

New York

Certified Chain of Custody
35% Certified Forest Content,
65% Certified Sourcing
www.sfiprogram.org
SFI-00993

reck-It Ralph was a Bad Guy. His job was to destroy things inside an arcade video game called Fix-It Felix, Jr.

As soon as the game started, Ralph began smashing buildings. "I'm gonna wreck it!"

Fix-It Felix was the hero of the game. He repaired everything that Ralph wrecked. "I can fix it!"

Every time a kid beat the game, Felix won a medal. Then the Nicelanders would yell at Ralph and throw him in the mud.

Ralph tried not to mind. After all, every game needed a Bad Guy.

One day, Ralph decided that he'd had enough. He snuck out of Fix-It Felix, Jr. and went into a video game called Hero's Duty. If Ralph got past all the evil cy-bugs and their eggs, he would win the Medal of Heroes.

Ralph was sure that would prove he was a Good Guy!
But just as Ralph grabbed the medal, a cy-bug attacked
him! They fell into an escape pod, and the ship's computer
came online.

Ralph and the cy-bug launched across the arcade. They crashed into another game called Sugar Rush. Everything there was made out of candy.

Ralph was upset. "Oh, no. This is that candy go-kart game over by the whack-a-mole!" Ralph managed to get free from the escape pod. But the cy-bug sank into a sea of taffy.

Meanwhile, the Nicelanders in Fix-It Felix, Jr. were in big trouble. Without Ralph wrecking things, kids thought the game was broken. A giant OUT OF ORDER sign was put on it.

Felix set out to find Ralph. "It is my job to fix what Ralph wrecks."

Back in Sugar Rush, Ralph realized his medal was missing. It had landed in a tree when the pod crashed. He started climbing.

"You're not from here, are you?" A little girl named Vanellope von Schweetz was also in the tree. She noticed Ralph's medal. "Sweet mother of monkey milk, a gold coin!"

Vanellope snatched the medal away from Ralph. She hurried to the other side of the kingdom. A kart race was about to begin.

King Candy was in charge. He explained the rules.

"The first nine racers across that finish line will represent Sugar Rush as tomorrow's avatars."

The entry fee for the race was one gold coin.

Vanellope ran up and tossed Ralph's golden medal into the entry pot. The crowd gasped.

"The glitch!"

Vanellope wanted to race more than anything. But she wasn't supposed to. There was a problem with her programming. Everyone thought that the arcade would put Sugar Rush out of order if she competed.

Just then, Ralph showed up. He had fallen into a taffy pool and was covered in sticky candy.

He chased Vanellope. "You! Give me back my medal right now!"

Ralph finally caught up to Vanellope. By that point, he
was clean from the taffy. Just before he reached Vanellope,
he overheard the other racers in Sugar Rush teasing her.
They threw her in the mud and smashed her kart!
That made Ralph angry. "Hey! Leave her alone!"

He chased the kids away.

Afterward, Vanellope told Ralph she had a plan. "You help me get a new kart, a real kart, and I'll win the race and get you back your medal."

Ralph reluctantly agreed. "You better win."

Meanwhile, Felix had tracked Ralph to Sugar Rush. He joined forces with Sergeant Calhoun from Hero's Duty. Calhoun wanted to make sure no cy-bugs had escaped from her game. Felix wanted to bring Ralph home so he couldn't "go Turbo."

Felix explained that when the arcade had first opened, Turbo was the star of a popular game called Turbo Time.

But when a newer, fancier game came to the arcade, Turbo was jealous. He took it over, and kids thought it was broken. Turbo ended up putting both games and himself out of order, for good. Felix needed to bring Ralph home, or the same thing would happen to his game.

On the other side of the kingdom, Ralph and Vanellope were busy baking a kart. It was very complicated. In the end, the kart turned out lumpy. And it was covered in crazy decorations. Ralph thought it was a disaster.

But Vanellope was thrilled. She finally had a real racing kart! When Ralph saw her face, he couldn't help feeling a little proud.

It was almost time for the race. Vanellope ran to get something. Just then, King Candy showed up—with Ralph's medal.

He explained that Vanellope was never meant to be in Sugar Rush. If she raced, kids would think the game had glitches. It would go out of order, and Vanellope would disappear . . . forever.

"I know it's tough. But heroes have to make the tough choices, don't they? She can't race, Ralph." The king offered to give Ralph his medal back as long as he promised to keep Vanellope from racing.

Ralph reluctantly agreed. He wanted Vanellope to stay safe.

King Candy left just as Vanellope returned. She had made
a special medallion for Ralph. It said, "YOU'RE MY HERO."

Ralph felt terrible. He had to tell her the bad news.
"Look, you can't be a racer."

Vanellope saw that Ralph had his medal back and thought
he had turned against her. "You're a rat, and I don't need
you, and I can win the race on my own."

Ralph realized there was only one way to keep Vanellope
from racing. He smashed her kart.

"You really are a bad guy." Vanellope ran off in tears.

Ralph sadly headed back to the Fix-It Felix, Jr. game. When he got there, he noticed something strange. Across the arcade he could see the Sugar Rush game console. It showed pictures of all the racers. And Vanellope was one of them!

Vanellope wasn't a glitch. King Candy had lied to him!

Ralph realized that King Candy had messed with Vanellope's programming. If Vanellope crossed the race's finish line, the game would reset and her programming would be restored. Ralph dashed back to Sugar Rush.

He found Felix trapped in King Candy's dungeon. Ralph begged him to repair Vanellope's broken kart.

"There's a little girl whose only hope is this kart. Please, Felix, fix it, and I promise I will never try to be good again."

Felix fixed the kart in no time. Together, the friends found Vanellope. They needed to get her to the race.

By the time they reached the
track, the competition had already
begun. Vanellope caught up with
the other karts lickety-split.

Soon she was neck-and-neck
with King Candy.

The king was furious. He tried to run Vanellope off
the track. King Candy banged into her . . . and then he
began to glitch.

He transformed into Turbo! The crowd screamed.
King Candy was really Turbo!

Suddenly, the ground exploded! Hundreds of cy-bugs crawled out. Ralph realized they were going to destroy Sugar Rush.

Just then, he had an idea. Cy-bugs were attracted to bright things. Ralph climbed to the top of a tall mountain and wrecked it. A bright stream of diet soda shot out.

The cy-bugs flew straight into the geyser and were vaporized! A cy-bug chomped Turbo and flew into the soda, too.

Ralph was about to fall in. Suddenly, Vanellope zoomed up on her kart. She rescued Ralph from the mountain just in time.

They were both heroes!

Back at the finish line, Vanellope climbed into her kart.
Ralph smiled. "You ready for this?"
Vanellope took a deep breath. "As ready as I'll ever be."
Ralph pushed her across the finish line. Then
something incredible happened. Vanellope's programming
was restored . . .

. . . and she transformed into a princess! It turned out Vanellope wasn't just a racer. She was the true leader of Sugar Rush.

Everyone cheered.

Ralph and Vanellope hugged good-bye. It was time for Ralph, Felix, and Calhoun to go home.

Back in Fix-It Felix, Jr., things were different for Ralph. The Nicelanders appreciated his wrecking, and they were much kinder to him. And Ralph decided that as long as he had Vanellope's friendship, he didn't need a medal to prove he was good, after all.

Because if a little girl like Vanellope liked him, how bad could he be?